The Crazy Quilt

Written by
Kristin Avery

Illustrated by
David McPhail

NOBLESVILLE CHRISTIAN SCHOOL
1835 N. TENTH STREET
NOBLESVILLE IN 46060

PROPERTY OF NCS LIBRARY

GoodYearBooks

NOBLESVILLE CHRISTIAN SCHOOL
1005 N. TENTH STREET
NOBLESVILLE IN 46060

Tanya found a quilt.
"What's this?" she asked her mother.

"It's a crazy quilt made from favorite clothes," said Tanya's mother.

Tanya pointed to a spot of gray.
"What's this from?" she asked.

"That's from Uncle's favorite coat,"
said her mother.

Tanya pointed to a spot of blue.
"What's this from?" she asked.

"That's from Grandpa's favorite shirt,"
said her mother.

Tanya pointed to a spot of red.
"What's this from?" she asked.

"That's from Grandma's favorite
skirt," said her mother.

Tanya had an idea.
She found her brother's favorite shirt.

She found her sister's favorite skirt.

She found her father's favorite tie.

She found her mother's favorite scarf.

The next morning,
her father said, "Where's my tie?"
Her brother said, "Where's my shirt?"

Her mother said, "Where's my scarf?"
Her sister said, "Where's my skirt?"

And Tanya said,
"Good morning! Do you like my
new crazy quilt?"